Note for the reader:-
Because I am more familiar with Yoruba names, I have used them in my story. It is not however based on any particular African customs, myths or costumes. When I was a child, I read and listened to many folk and fairy stories from all over the world, including my country, Nigeria. This is my own story, put together from memories of those which have stayed with me.

Carol Olu Easmon

For my late dear friend Ananda Raja and my nephew Marlon. Also for Charles, Sada Shiva, my father and my late mother. For my brothers and sister, my Ghana family and my children – Omar – Marimba and Adeyemi.

First American edition published in 1990 by
Crocodile Books, USA
An imprint of Interlink Publishing Group, Inc.
99 Seventh Avenue • Brooklyn, New York 11215

Library of Congress Cataloging-in-Publication Data
Easmon, Carol.
   Bisi and the golden disc / Carol Olu Easmon.
      p.   cm.
   "First American edition" ——T.p. verso.
   Summary: When an evil sorcerer changes her true love into a blue snake, Bisi comes to his rescue with the aid of a magic disc.
   ISBN 0-940793-56-3
   [1. Fairy tales.   2. Africa——Fiction.]   I. Title.
PZ8.E12674B1   1990
[Fic]——dc20   89-77347
                                                          CIP
                                                          AC

Printed and bound by
Printer Portuguesa, Portugal

BISI AND THE GOLDEN DISC

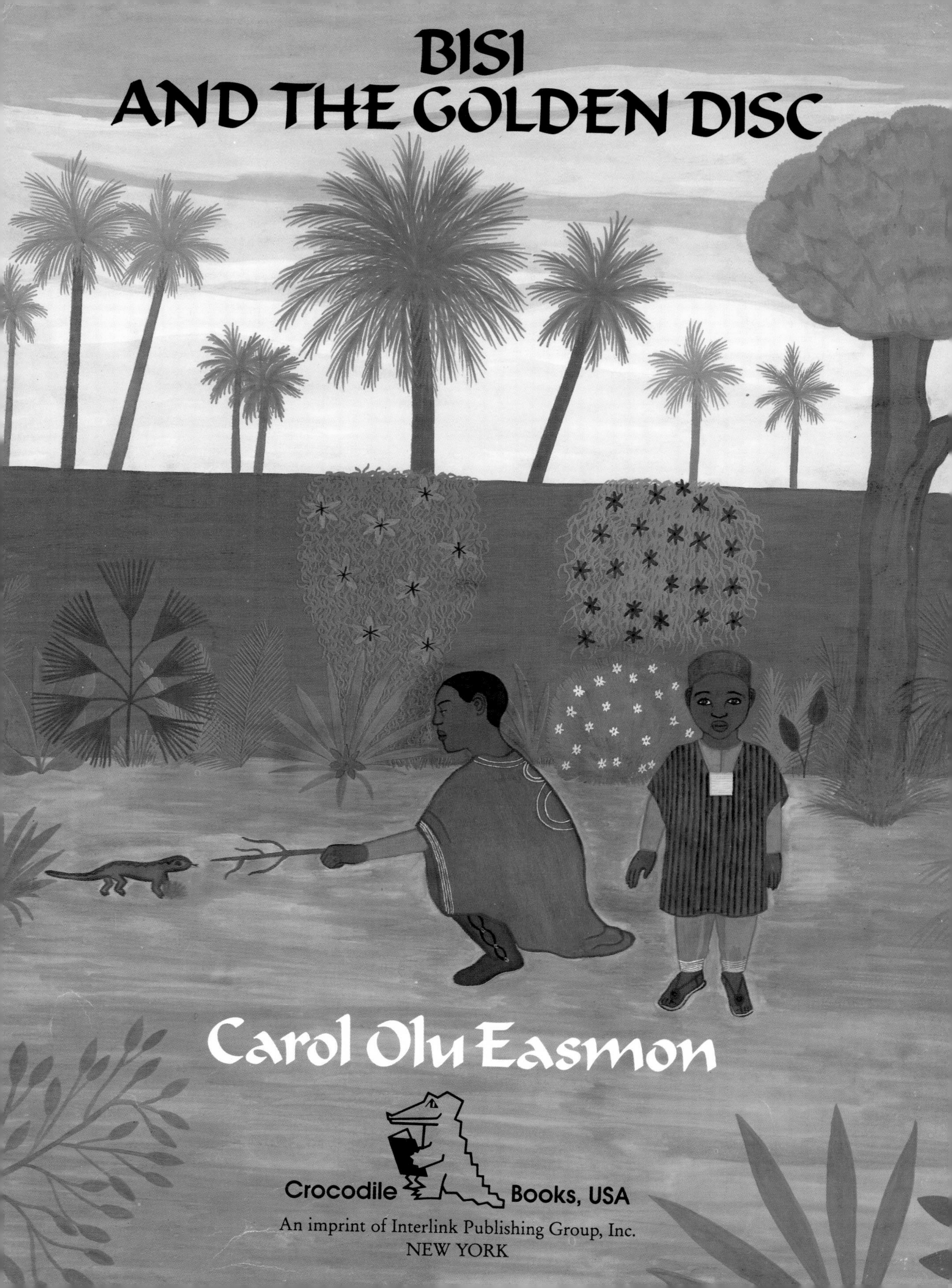

Carol Olu Easmon

Crocodile Books, USA
An imprint of Interlink Publishing Group, Inc.
NEW YORK

Once upon a time there was a king in Africa whose name was Olu. He had a daughter named Bisi, and two sons, Adeyemi and Adebiyi. Parents should love their children equally, but King Olu had a favorite, his daughter Bisi. She reminded him of her mother, who had died giving birth to Adebiyi.

It was the custom at that time for kings to marry many women, but King Olu never had. He had been quite happy with one wife, and wanted his daughter to be the only wife of her chosen husband. But despite his independent mind and tender heart, King Olu did have a fault. He was very greedy.

Bisi had six attendants who had been with her since she was a child. They were like sisters to her.

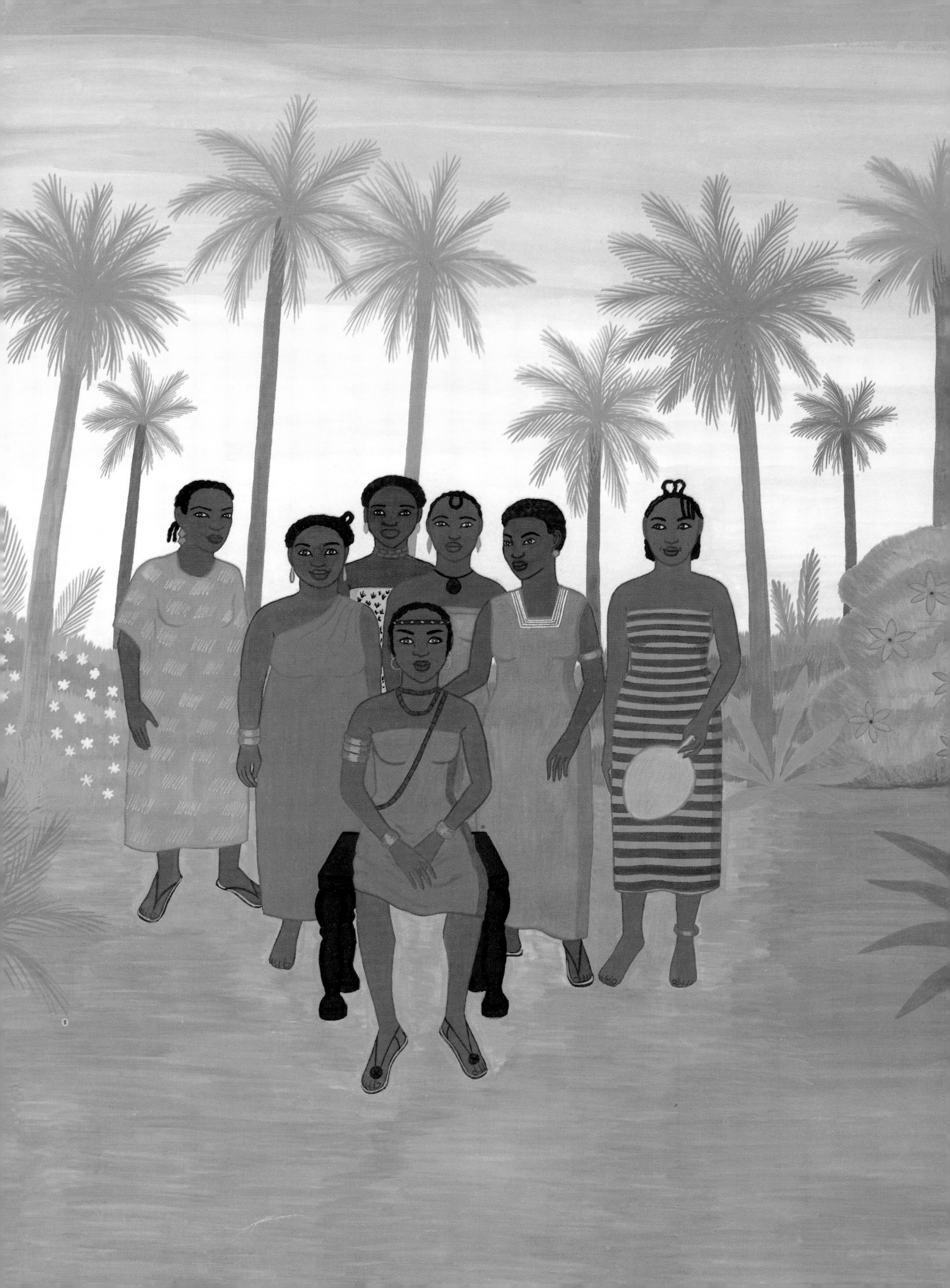

One hot day, Bisi and her attendants went to a nearby river to cool themselves. They swam and splashed in the cool water for a while, then came out and spread their cloths on the ground in the shade. For some time they gossiped happily, giggling about the goings on at the Palace, until suddenly, loud shouts and noisy laughter caught their attention. A group of young men were wrestling and swimming in the water. One in particular caught Bisi's eye. He was tall and proud looking. His skin was like smooth brown velvet, his eyes were bright and clear and, when he smiled, his teeth were like the most exquisite pearls. He noticed Bisi gazing at him and called to her, but Bisi suddenly became shy and her heart beat like a drum.
She left the river, but sent one of her attendants to find out his name.
It was Akin.

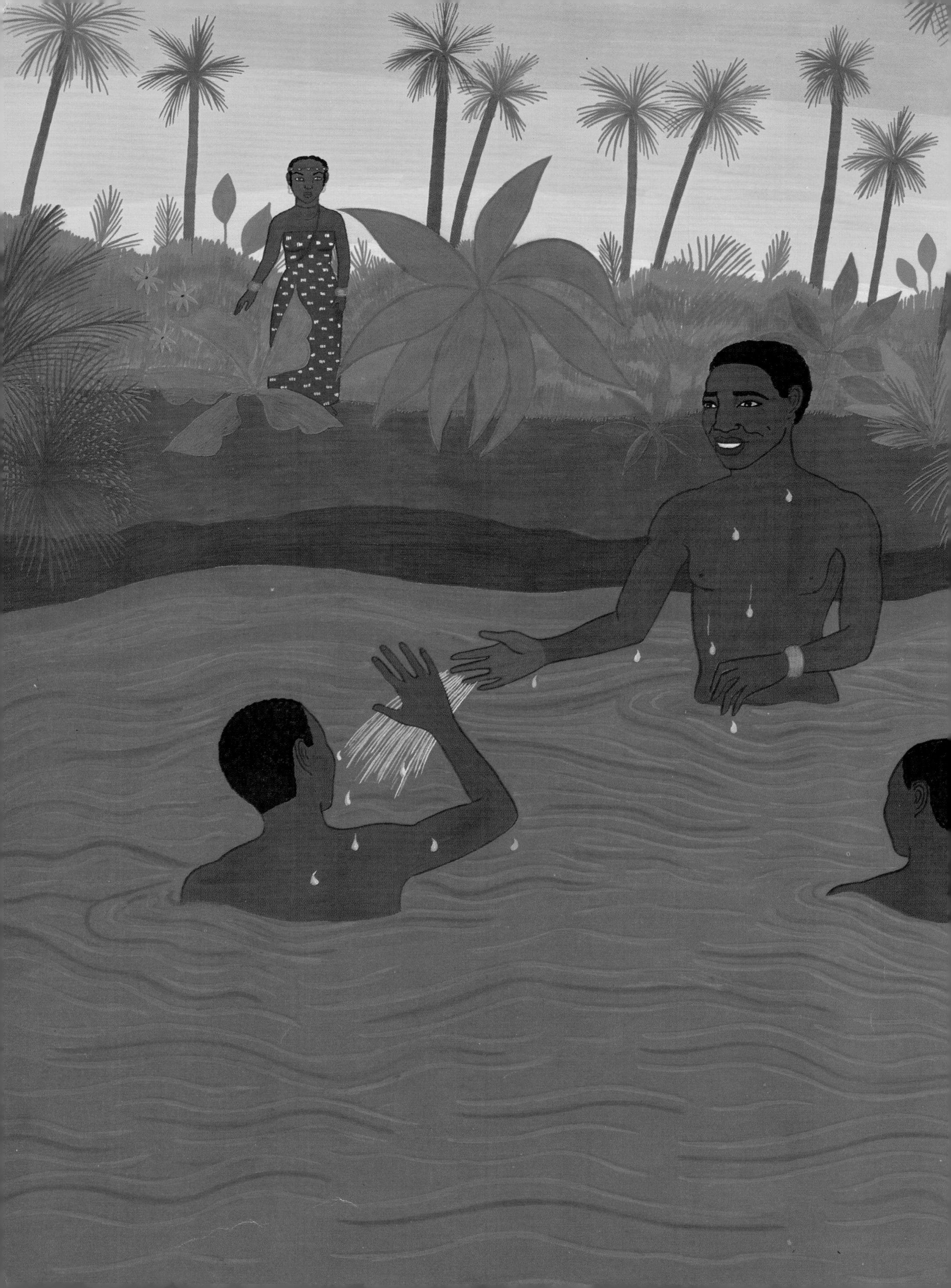

As they walked back to the Palace, Bisi and her attendants met a group of angry villagers who were chasing an old woman. They said she had been stealing food.

"If this is true," thought Bisi, "then she must be hungry."

So she took the old woman back to the Palace, where she was fed and comforted, then given a place to sleep for the night. The old woman thanked Bisi again and again for her kindness.

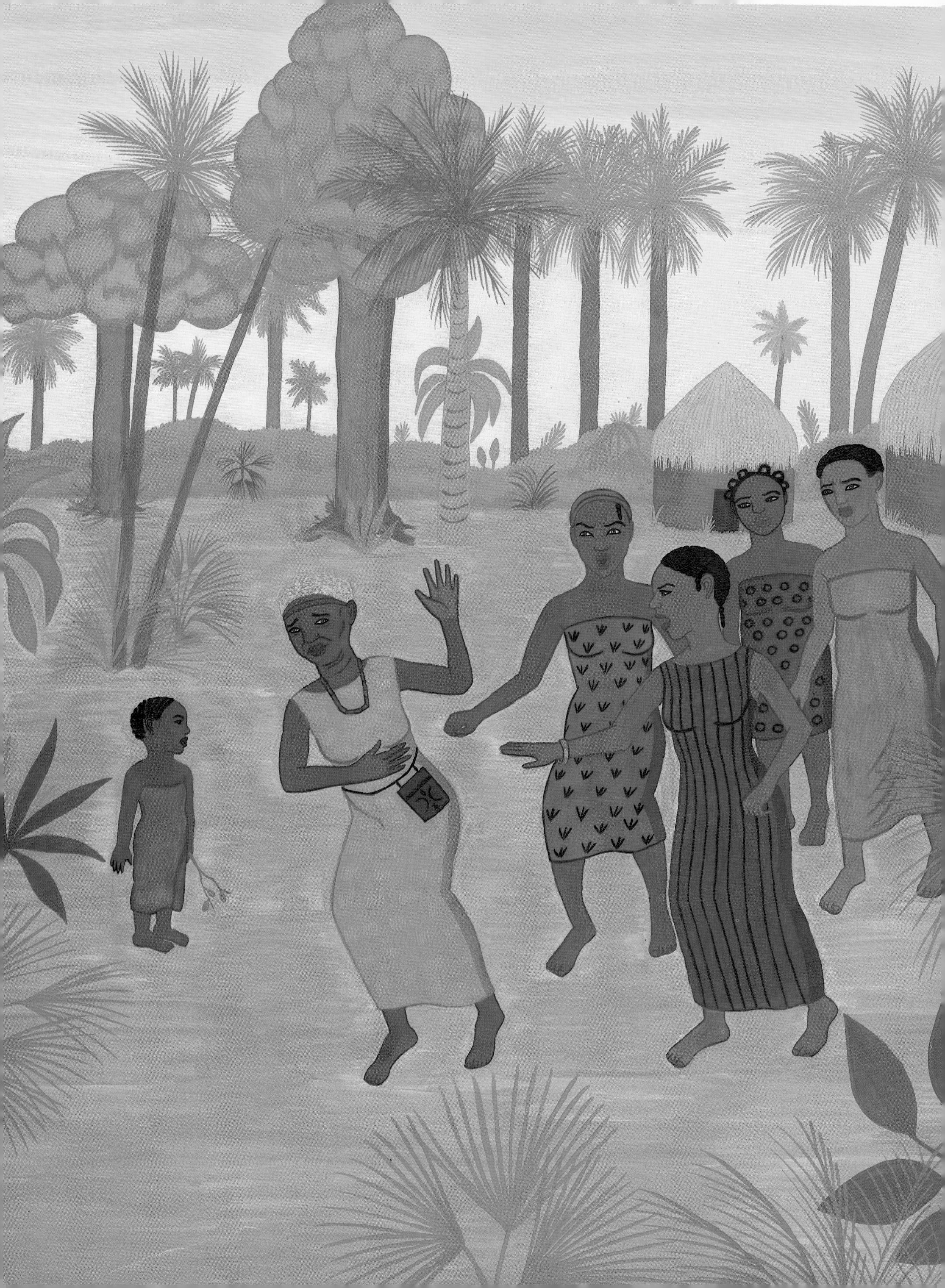

The next morning, Bisi went to see how the old woman was, but she had gone. On her bed she had left a beautiful golden disc. It was decorated with strange engravings, and in its center was a large red stone which sparkled in the early morning sunlight. Bisi sent one of her attendants for a chain from her jewelry chest. She put the disc on the chain and hung it around her neck, saying that she would not take it off until she saw the old woman again.

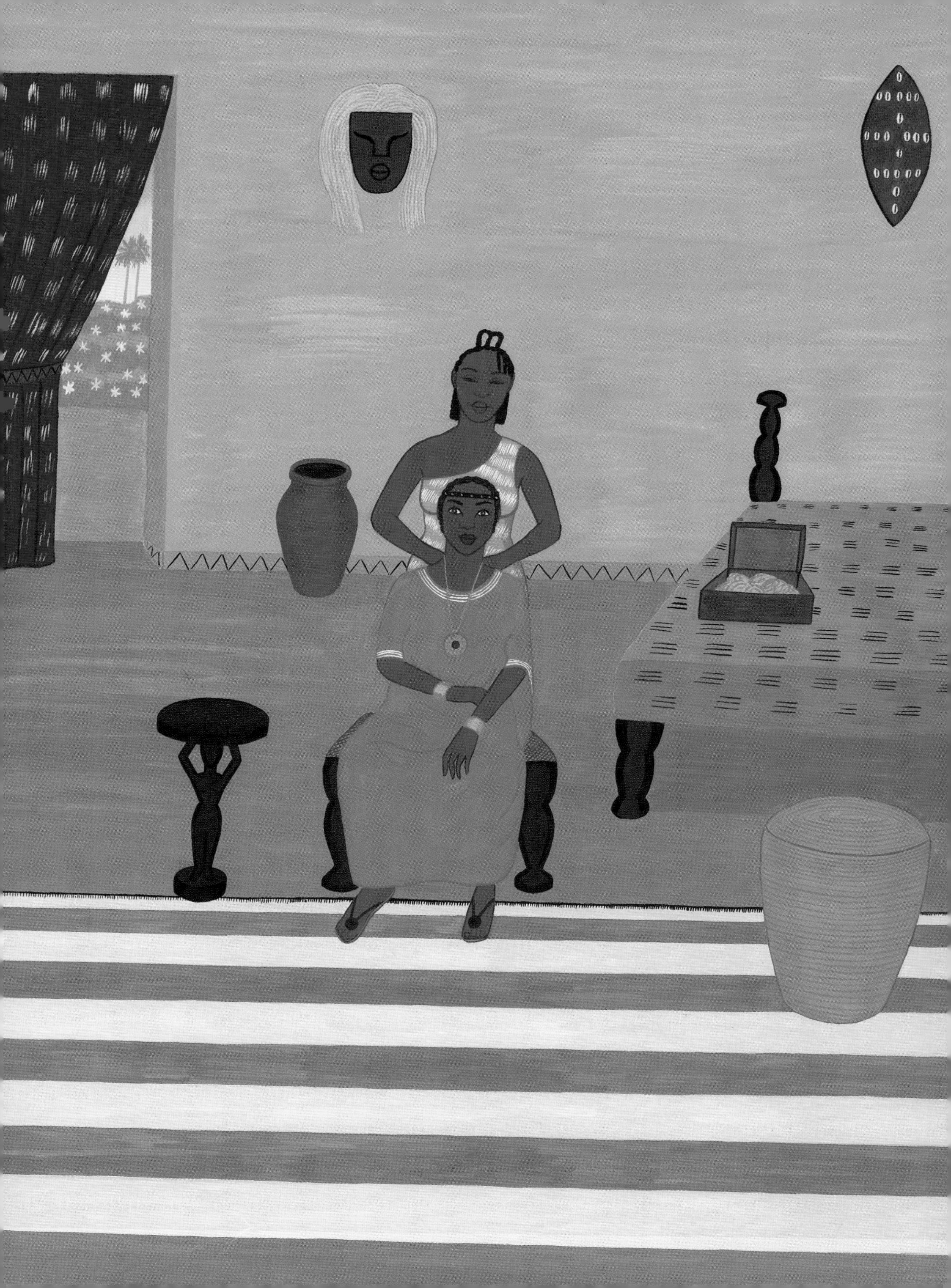

Deep in the forest of Olu's kingdom there lived an evil magician, whose name was Ogun. His hut was made of baked clay, and the roof was thatched with dried palm leaves. Inside, the walls were hung with snake and animal skins; skulls, bones, feathers and shells were scattered everywhere, as were little clay pots of colored powders. Ogun was very fierce, and very cunning, and he wanted to marry Bisi.

He had first seen her on one of his excursions to the river to gather plants for his spells, and was determined to get her father's consent to the marriage.

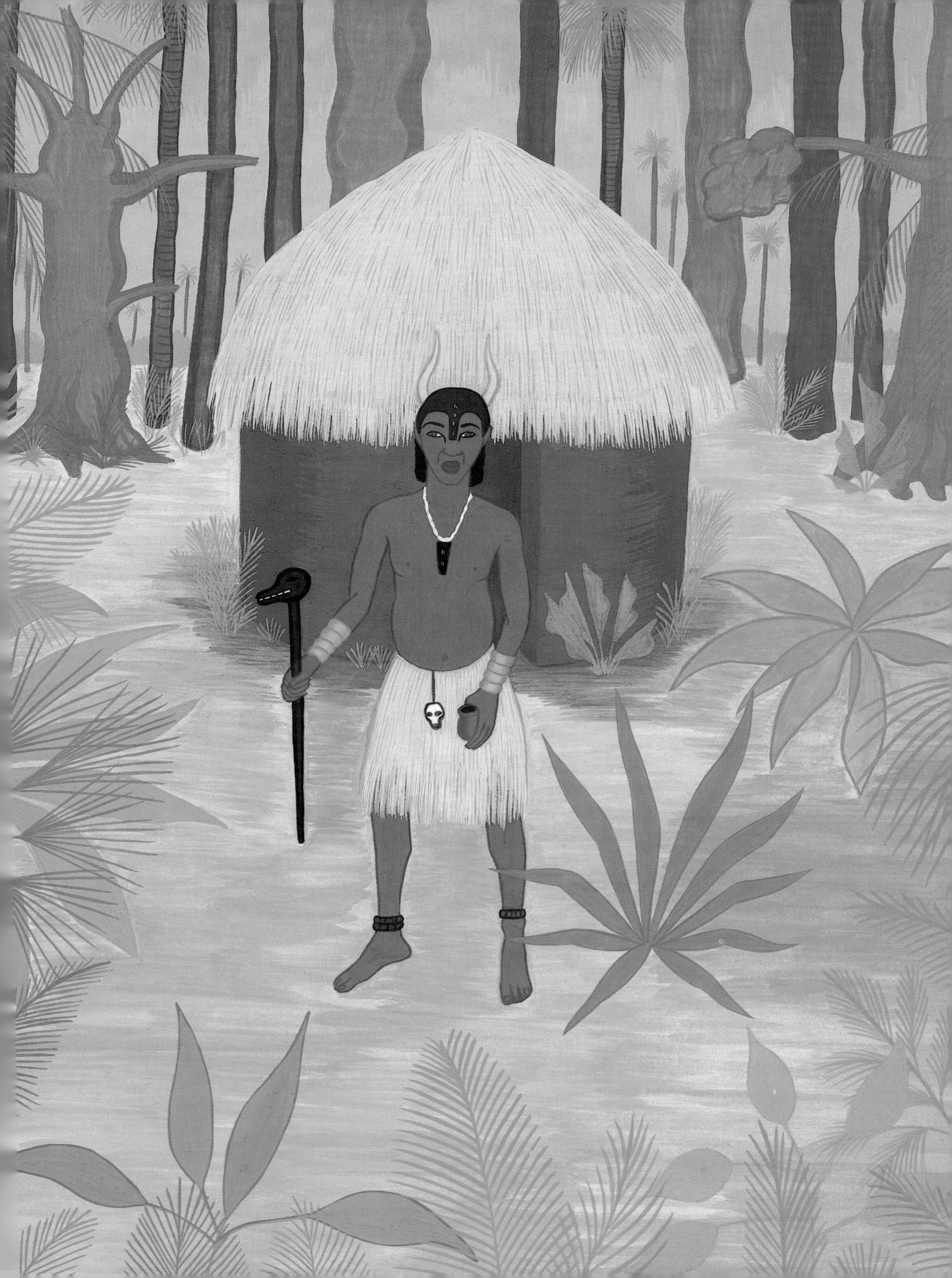

Through his magical powers, Ogun knew of King Olu's one weakness, his greed. He also knew that, to the north of the kingdom there lived a wealthy king named Bayo, whose lands King Olu would dearly love to add to his own, but he was not confident enough to make an attack. Ogun went to the king and promised that, if he were allowed to marry Bisi, he would use magic to make Olu ruler of Bayo's kingdom. Although King Olu loved Bisi very much, his greed was too great and he yielded to Ogun's temptation.

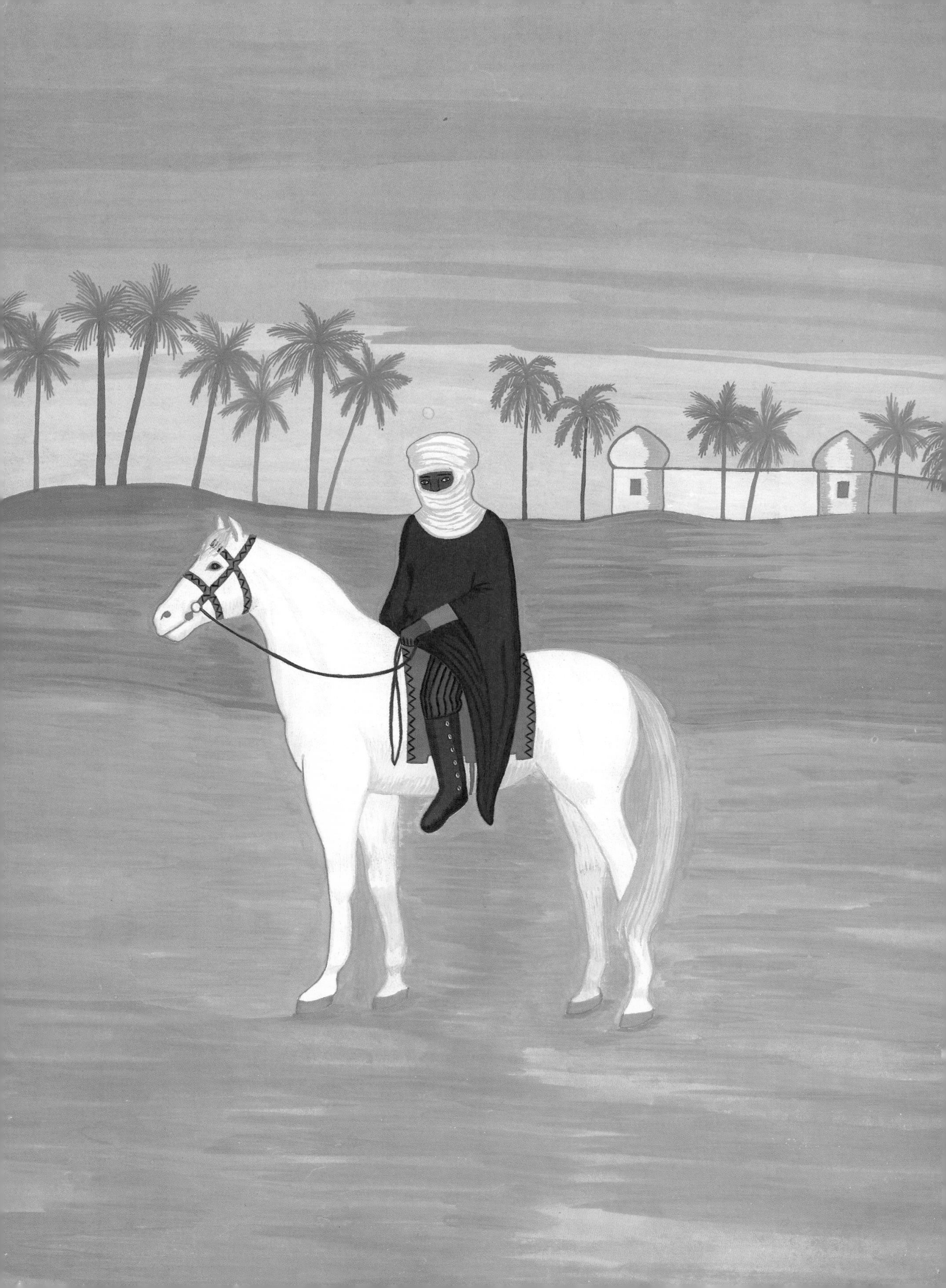

Meanwhile, Bisi was going regularly to the river to meet Akin. After she had overcome her initial shyness she felt as if she had always known him. They fell deeply in love, and at last decided that the time had come for Akin's father to go to the king and ask for his daughter's hand in marriage. Bisi was overjoyed. Next day, dressed in his finest clothes, Akin's father went to the king. Everyone in the kingdom knew that the princess would be allowed to marry the man of her choice, so he was not unduly worried. Though his family were not very wealthy, they were honest and brave. But King Olu did not give his consent, instead he played for time, telling Akin's father that certain rituals had to be performed before an official announcement could be made. Akin's father trusted the king and left, his heart filled with happiness.

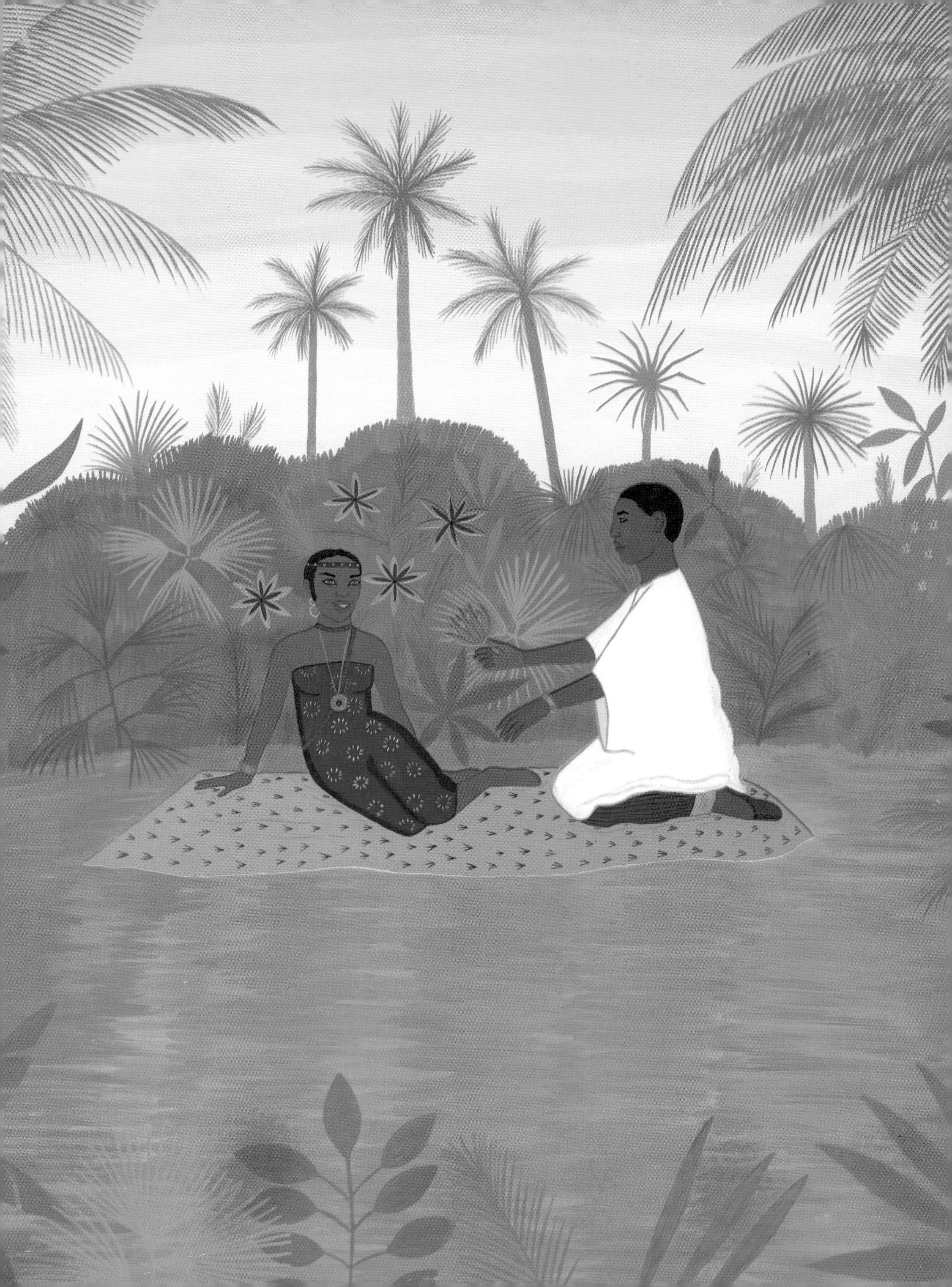

Ogun, sitting at home, had seen all that happened by means of a powerful spell. The next morning, armed with a large basket and one of his pots of powder, he set off for Akin's house and hid in the bushes. Soon Akin appeared, for it was his custom to hunt alone in the mornings. As he came near the bushes, Ogun sprang out and, before Akin realized what was happening, threw blue powder in his face, causing him to choke, and blinding him. Then, an even more terrible thing happened. Akin was transformed into a hideous blue snake. Quick as a flash, Ogun scooped the snake up from the ground and stuffed it into his basket. He took it across the river and released it into the forest. Satisfied, he went to see King Olu to tell him what he had done. The King was full of remorse when he heard Ogun's story. But Ogun was ready for this.

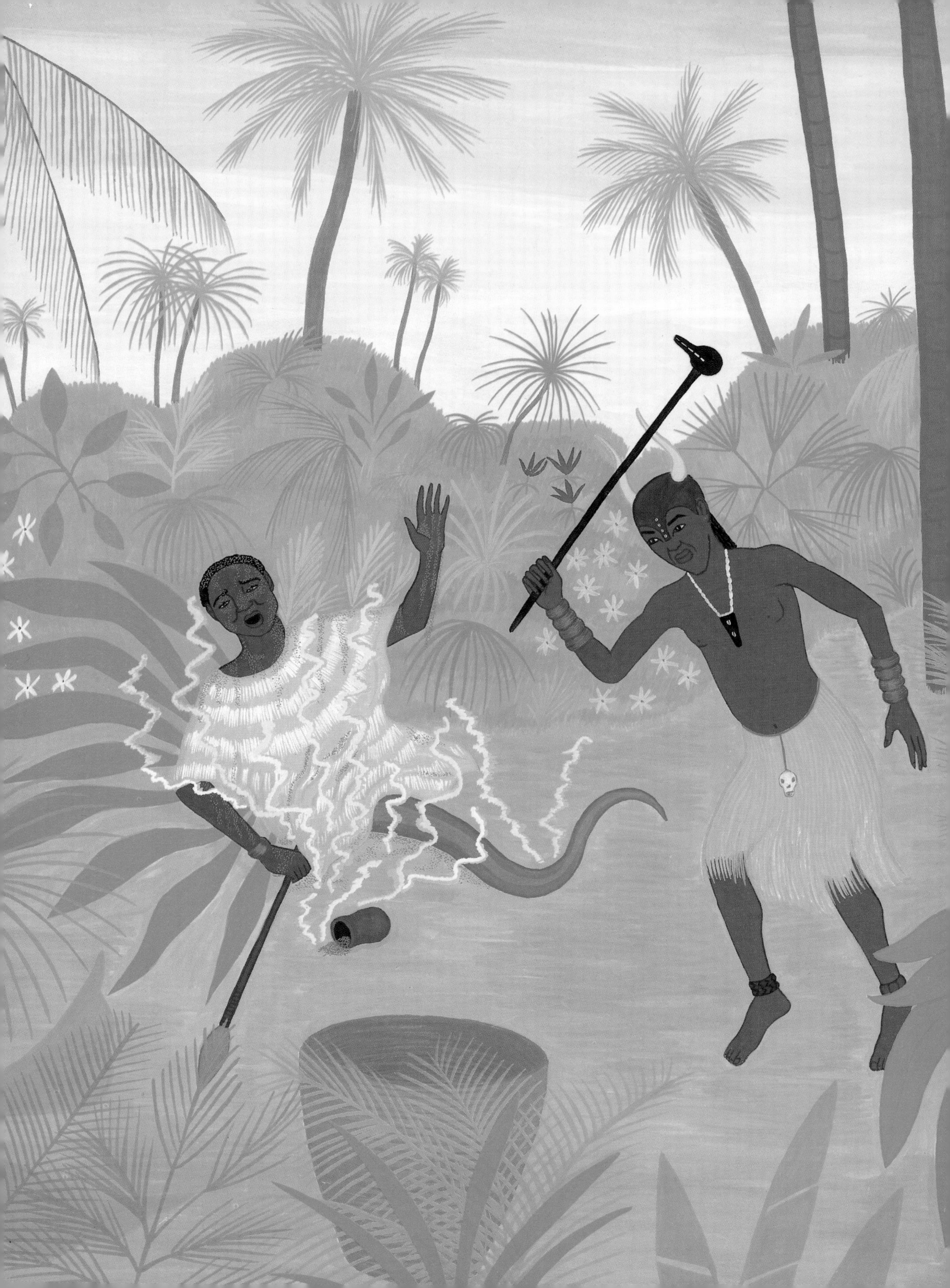

He called for a calabash of water, then, after asking the king to dismiss his attendants, he passed his hand over the water, muttering strange words unfamiliar to King Olu. As the king watched the water, to his amazement pictures began to form. He saw gold ornaments, carvings and richly woven cloths.

"This," said Ogun, "represents only a tiny fraction of Bayo's wealth."

Any qualms King Olu had were quickly dispelled. He agreed to Ogun's next plan.

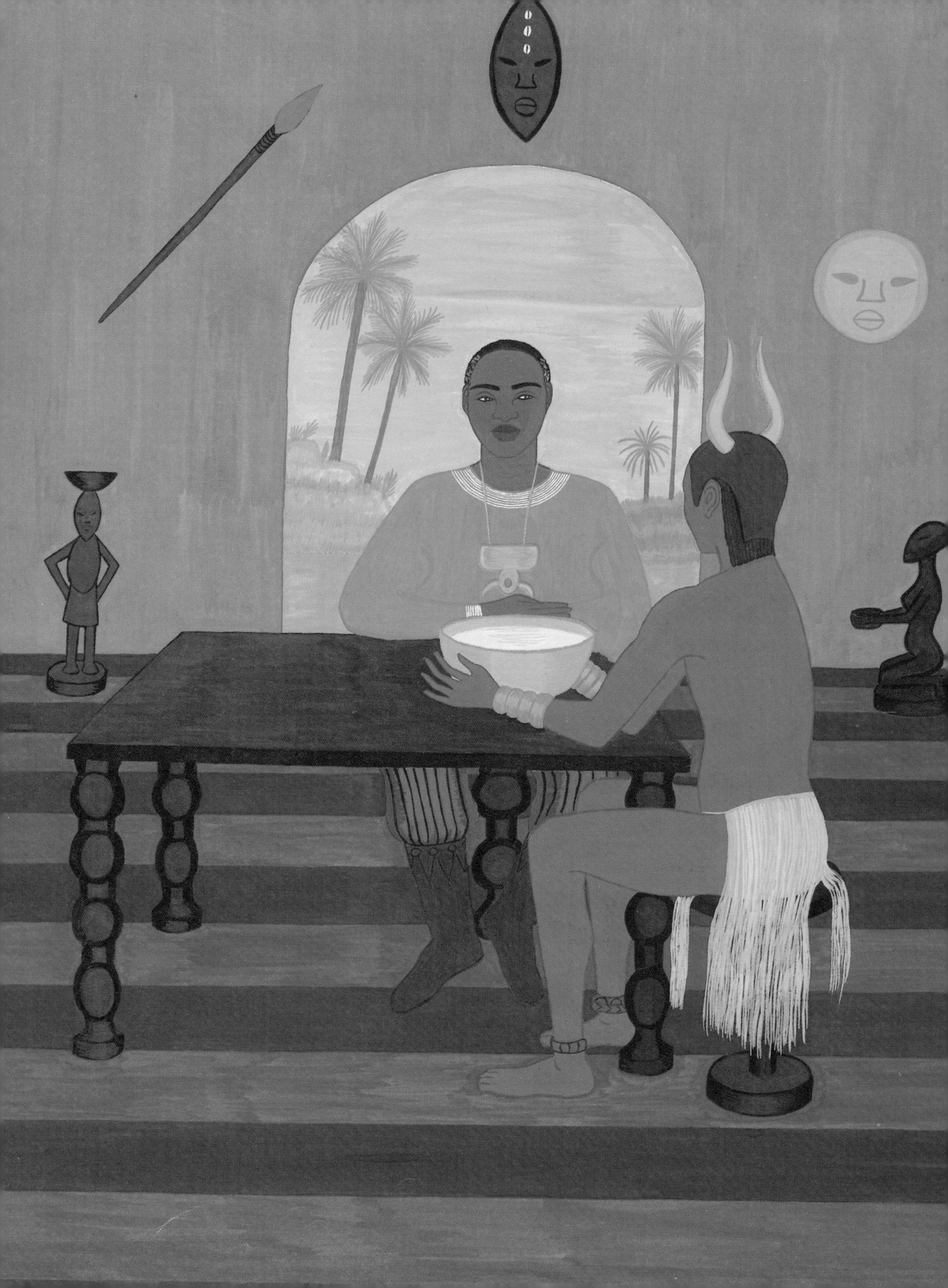

Bisi waited all that evening for her father to call her and discuss her wedding, but no call came. All the next day she waited, until at last she could bear it no longer and went to see him. She told him how much she loved Akin and how she wanted to marry him. She asked if the necessary arrangements had been made with his father. King Olu was most distressed and, for a brief moment, thought of abandoning his plans, but when he thought of Bayo's kingdom and Ogun's wrath, his good intentions faded. At last, the king spun a web of deceit, telling Bisi that if she could find the blue snake in the forest and kill it, she could marry her love. If she failed, she would have to marry Ogun.

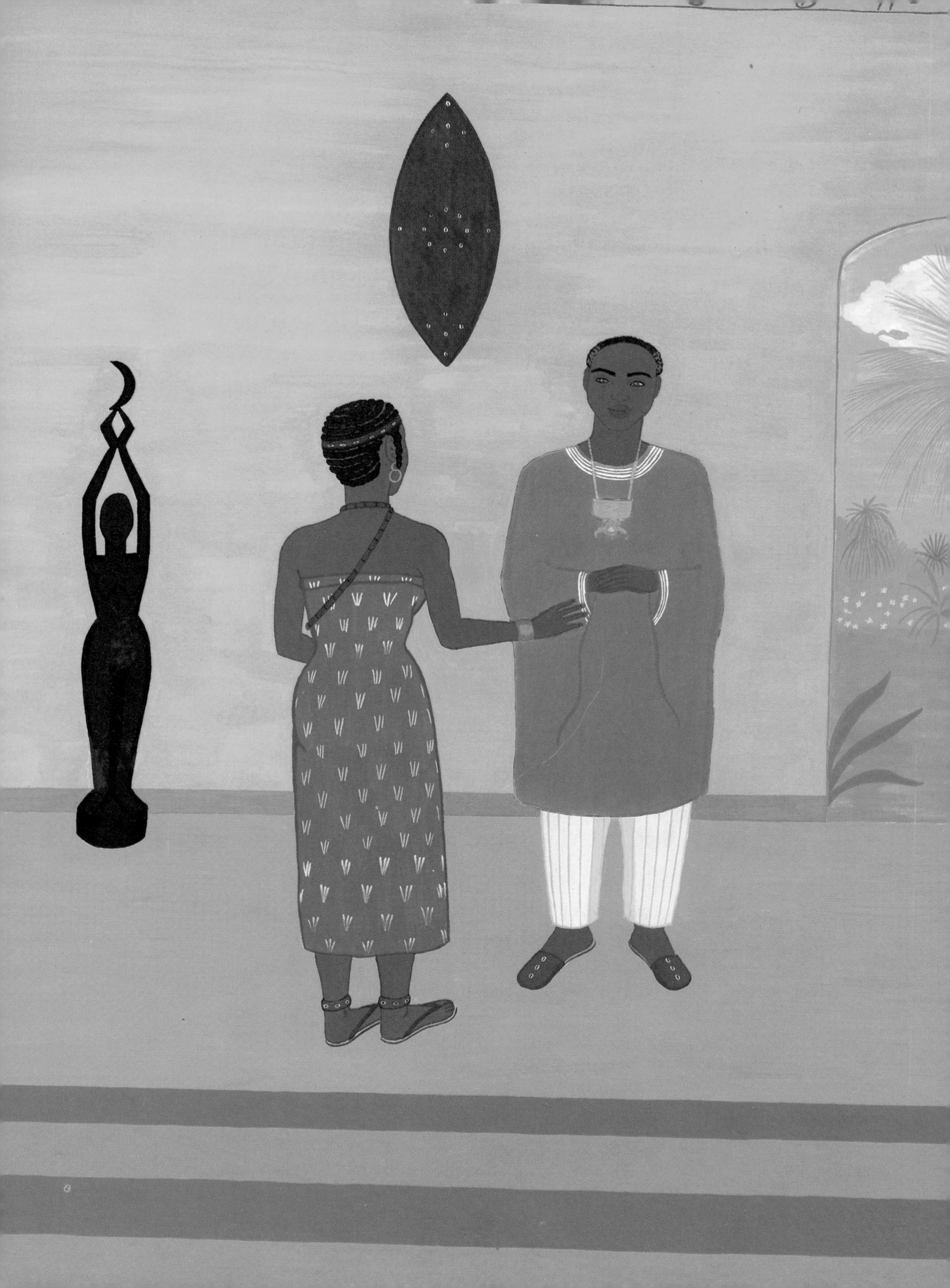

Bisi readily agreed, and immediately began preparing for her journey. She called her attendants and ordered them to pack food, medicines, fresh clothes and arm themselves with her brother's spears. Then they set off. Bisi and her attendants crossed the river and made their way towards the forest, asking any passers by if they had seen a strange blue snake. Nobody had. When darkness fell, they settled down to sleep.

The next morning, they were awakened by shouts and screams. A woman came hurtling out of the forest with a young child in her arms. She was terrified. When Bisi had calmed her, she asked her what the matter was. The woman told her that, after a scolding, her child had run off into the forest. When she went to bring him back, she had seen a blue snake. Bisi did not hesitate. She and her helpers picked up their spears and rushed off in the direction that the distraught woman had indicated. They had gone only a short way when they saw the snake, coiled around the base of a palm tree, almost as if it were waiting for them.

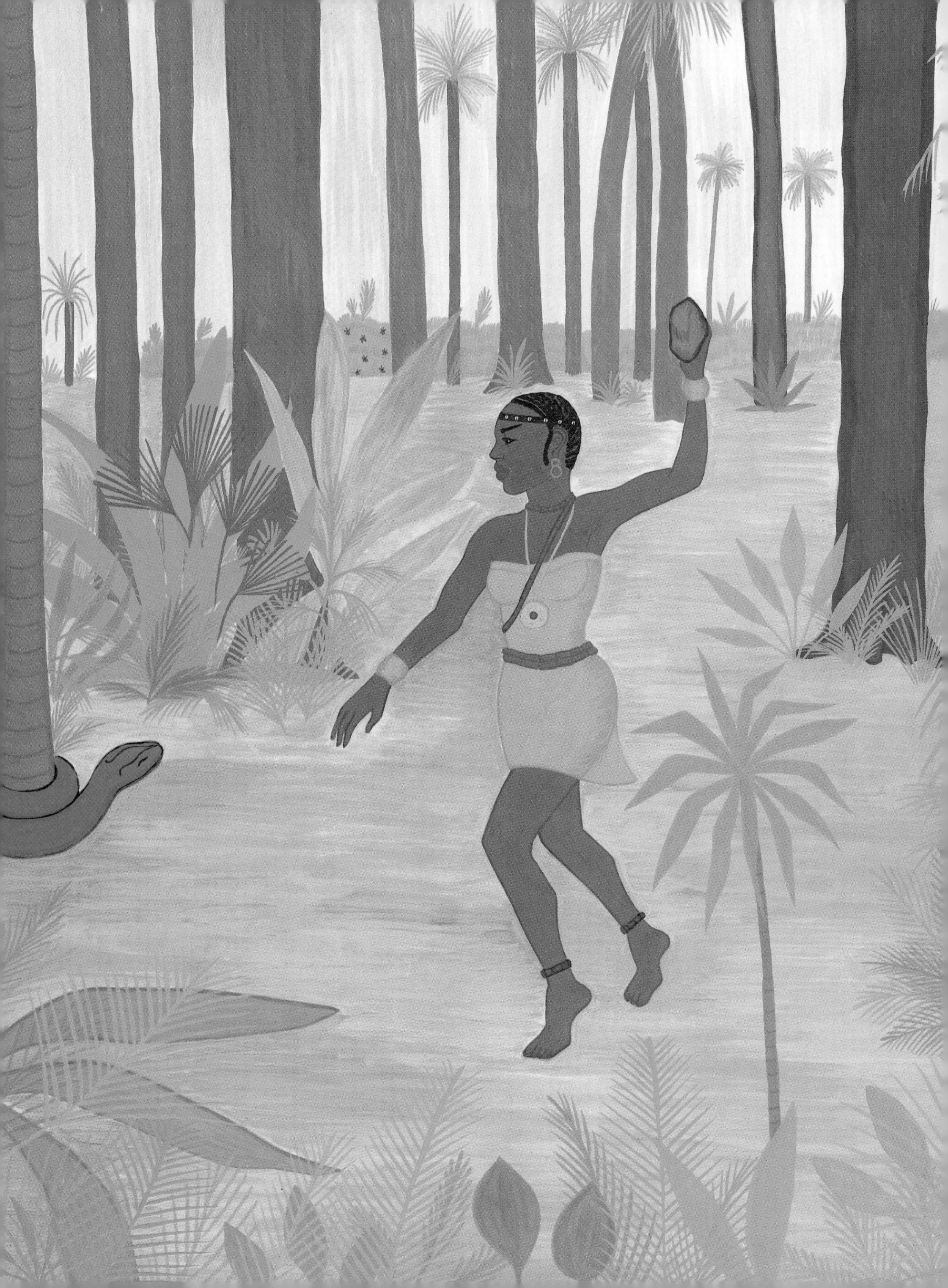

One of the attendants said that it would probably be best to crush the reptile's head with a rock, rather than attempt to use a spear.

Bisi stepped on silent feet toward the snake, feeling a little sorry for it because her heart was soft. It seemed wrong to kill a sleeping creature. But resolutely she lifted the rock in her hand, high above her head, and was about to bring it down on the creature's head when the golden disc slipped from the chain around her neck. A shaft of light flashed from the stone in the disc and dazzled her eyes. For a moment she was blinded. When her vision cleared, there stood the old woman who left her the disc.

"Do not harm the snake, Bisi," the old woman commanded. "It is Akin, your love." She began to hum a strange tune. The serpent rose up, then stayed still. The old woman picked up the disc from the ground and passed it along the snake's head, down along the length of its body, and off over its tail.

A strange silence descended over the forest and it was filled with a gentle golden mist. There, where the snake had been, stood Akin. Bisi rushed to embrace him and they cried like small children.

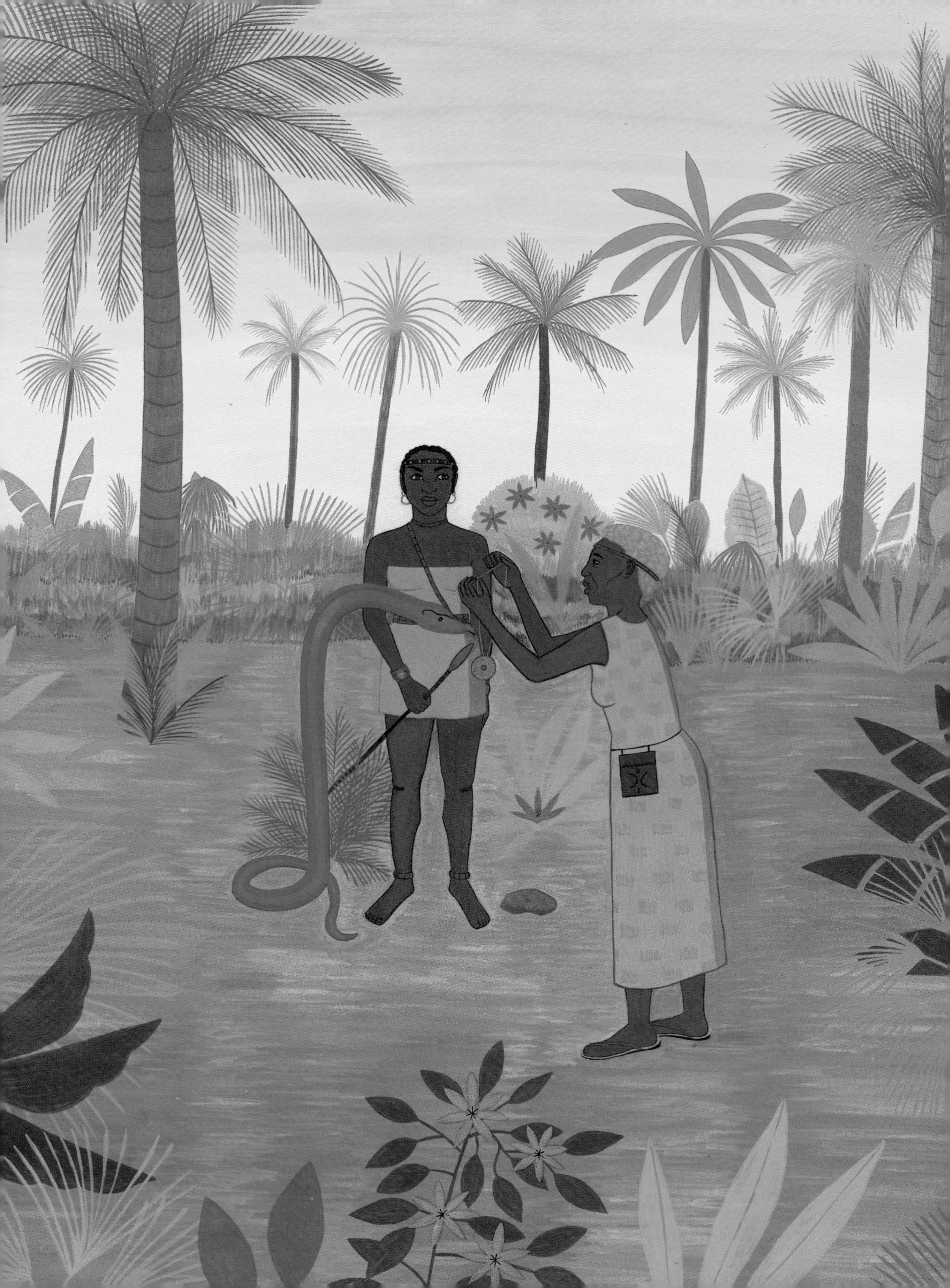

When they had recovered, the old woman explained what had happened, beseeching Bisi to forgive her father, because he was strongly influenced by Ogun's evil powers. Bisi and Akin returned to the Palace, where they found the king and his whole household trembling with fear. Ogun had seen a vision that his plans had been thwarted, and had come to seek revenge. At that very moment he was weaving a spell. He threw powder on the ground and the sky darkened as if a terrible storm was approaching. The earth shook. Then the old woman ran forward shouting Ogun's name. As he turned to look at her, she held up the golden disc.

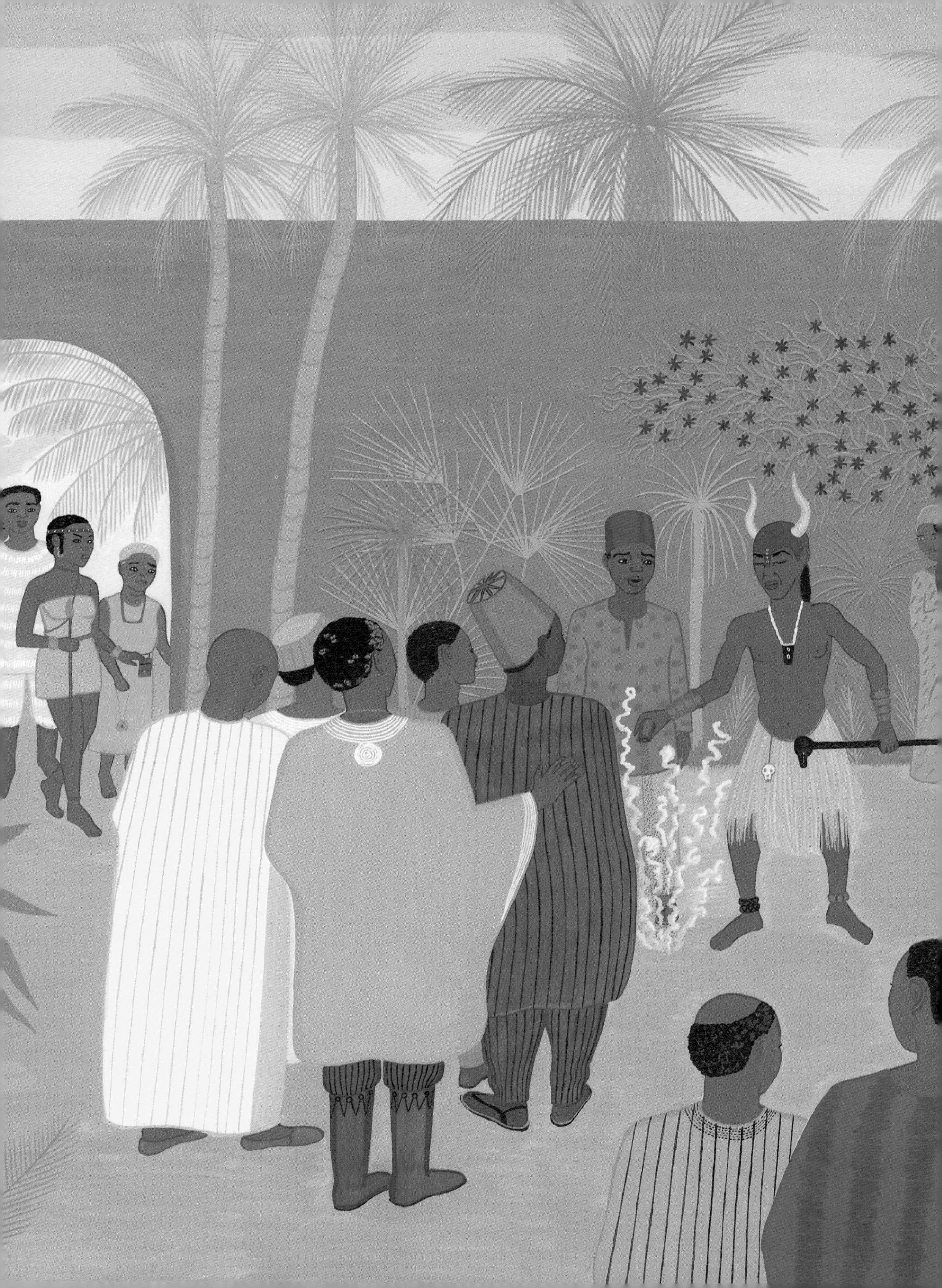

A strong red light shone from its center and, with a sound like the rushing of a mighty wind, the magician was sucked screaming into the disc. Everybody shouted with joy and relief.

The old woman promised that now the disc had done its work she would destroy it and use her magic only for the good of the whole kingdom. Akin's family were filled with joy when they saw him again, because they had thought him killed by some wild beast in the forest.

At first, King Olu could not share in the general happiness, for he was filled with remorse. But Bisi forgave her father, and the very next day, the king ordered preparations for the wedding to begin.

Amidst much joy and celebration, the wedding took place. The air was filled with the thudding of drums and happy laughter. King Olu even invited Bayo, the king from the North – indeed, kings from all over Africa. Bisi's wedding was the beginning of a long period of peace among all the kingdoms of Africa.

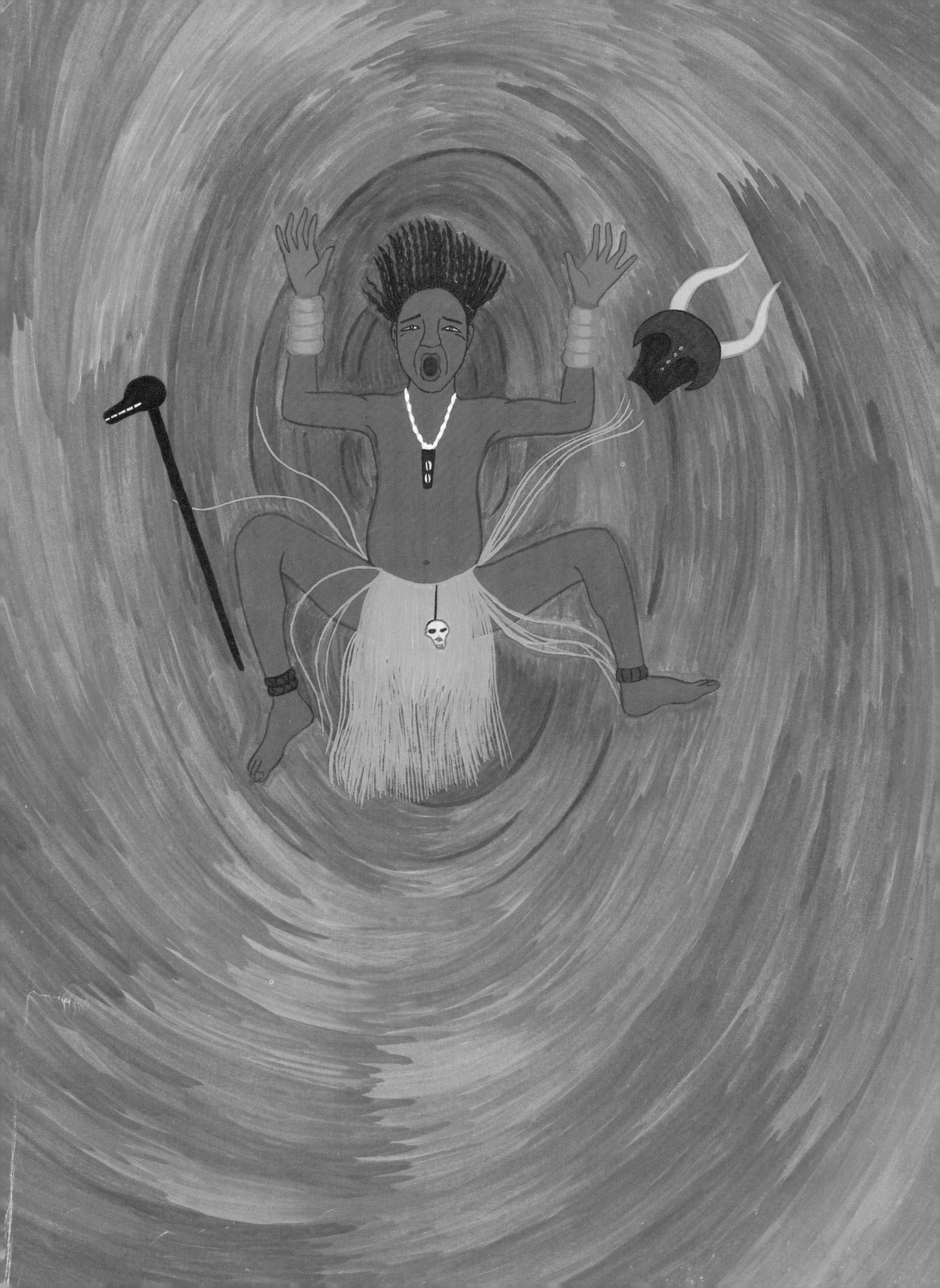

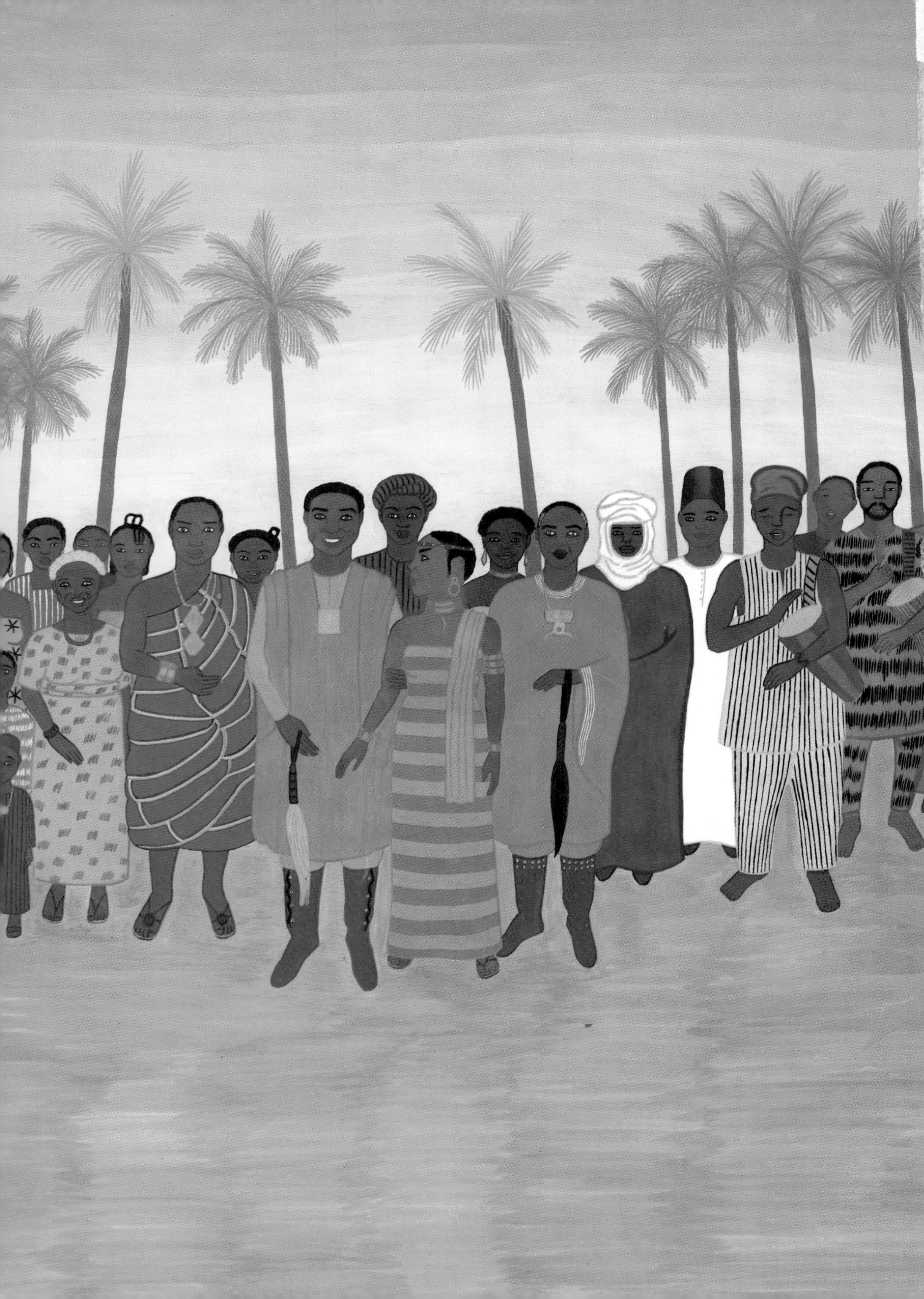